To ....

For being good.

MERRY CHRISTMAS!

From Santa

Santa is coming to Australia

Written by Steve Smallman
Illustrated by Robert Dunn
Designed by Sarah Allen

ALicat
Alicat Publishing
16 Sandilands Street
South Melbourne VIC 3205
Australia
Email: publishing@alicat.com.au
www.alicat.com.au
Printed in China 5 4 3 2
AC13 377

Santa is coming to Australia

Written by Steve Smallman

Illustrated by Robert Dunn

ALicat

"Well?"

boomed Santa. "Have all the children from **Australia** been good this year?"

"Well...uh...mostly," answered the little old elf, as he bustled across the busy workshop to Santa's desk.

Santa peered down at the elf from behind the tall, teetering piles of letters that the children of Australia had sent him.

"Mostly?" asked Santa, looking over the top of his glasses.

"Yes...but they've all been **especially** good in the last few days!" said the elf.

"Jolly good!" chuckled Santa,
"Then we'd better get their presents loaded up!"

Even though the sack of presents was

really, really big

and the elves were **really, really** small,

they seemed to have no trouble loading it onto Santa's sleigh.
Though how they managed to fit such a big sack into one little sleigh
even they didn't know. But somehow they did.

"Splendid!" boomed Santa. "We're ready to go!"

"Er...not quite, Santa," said the little old elf. "One of our reindeer is missing!"

"Missing?

Which reindeer is missing?" asked Santa.

"The youngest one, Santa," said the elf. "It's his first flight tonight. I've called him and called him, but..."

Just then, a young reindeer strolled up, munching on a large carrot.

"where have you been?"

asked Santa.

But the youngest reindeer was crunching so loudly that it was no wonder he hadn't heard the little old elf calling.

"Oh well, never mind," said Santa, giving the reindeer a little wink. He took out his Santa-nav and tapped in the coordinates for Australia. **"This will guide us to Australia in no time."**

Crunch!
Crunch!
Crunch!

With a flick of the reins and
a jerk of the harness, off they
went, racing through the sky.

"Ho, ho, ho!"
laughed Santa.

"We'll soon have these presents
delivered to every little Aussie!"

Santa's sleigh flew through the starry night heading south. On they flew as the crisp, wintry night turned to daylight. In the wink of an eye, the sleigh crossed over the Equator and headed down under. The youngest reindeer was very excited. He had never been away from the North Pole before.

They had just crossed the coast in the Kimberleys
when, suddenly they ran into thick cloud.

They couldn't see a thing!

The youngest reindeer was getting a bit worried,
but Santa didn't seem worried at all.

"In two kilometres..."

said the Santa-nav in a bossy lady's voice,

"...keep left at the next star."

"But, madam," Santa blustered, "I can't see any stars in all this cloud!"
Soon they were

hopelessly lost!

Bong-bong!
Bong-bong!

Then, through the heavy cloud, the youngest reindeer heard a faint, chiming sound.

Bong-bong!

He looked over at the old reindeer with the red nose. But he had his head down.

(Red nose...I wonder who that could be?!)

Bong-bong!
Bong-bong!

Bong-bong! Bong-bong!

There was that sound again, like a clock chiming. The youngest reindeer turned around to look at Santa. But Santa wasn't listening. He seemed to be arguing with a little box with buttons on it.

With a flick of the harness and a jerk of the reins, the youngest reindeer gave a sharp *tug* and headed off towards the sound of the bells, pulling Santa and his sleigh behind him!

"Whoa!"

cried Santa, pulling his hat straight. "What's going on?" Then, to his surprise, he heard the chiming sound.

"Well done, young reindeer!" he shouted cheerfully, "It must be the Bell Tower in Perth. Don't worry, children, Santa is coming!"

Then, suddenly...

CRUNCH!

The sleigh hit something as it plummeted through the cloud. **"You have arrived!"** said the Santa-nav unhelpfully.

Finally, when the clouds parted, Santa discovered where 'arrived' was...

...stuck, right at the very top of
Central Park Tower!

"Everybody,
PULL!"

The reindeer *pulled* with all their might until, at last, with a screeching noise, the sleigh scraped clear of the tower and Santa steered them safely over the Swan River, past the Town Hall until he could stop safely in Kings Park.

Luckily, there was no
real damage done, but
the packages had all been
jumbled up. Santa quickly sorted
the presents into order again.

"All right," said Santa. "Thanks to this
young reindeer I know where we are
now. Don't worry, children,

Santa is coming!"

Santa drove his sleigh expertly from rooftop to rooftop all over Australia, popping in and out of chimneys as fast as he could go.

(who pretty fast for a chubby fellow!)

It didn't matter how big the chimneys were, or even if the home had a chimney, Santa worked at the speed of lightning, placing presents under every Christmas tree.

The youngest reindeer was
amazed at how quickly they
went. Santa never seemed to get
tired at all! And it looked like the
children in Australia were going
to be very lucky this year! But
the youngest reindeer was
starting to feel a bit weary
and quite hungry too!

He piled them under the Christmas trees
and carefully filled up the stockings
with surprises.

In house after house, Santa delved
inside his sack for packages of
every shape and size.

Santa took a little bite out of each cookie, a tiny sip of milk, wiped his beard, and popped the carrots into his sack.

In house after house, the good children of Australia had left out a plate of cookies, a small glass of milk and a big, crunchy carrot.

Australia is a big country, so Santa sped from Perth to Adelaide, up to Alice Springs, then on to Melbourne. Making sure he didn't forget Tasmania, he then headed north to Canberra, Sydney, Brisbane and Cairns, finally ending up in Darwin. Santa and his sleigh visited every house in Australia.

Santa delivered presents to Andrew, Anson, Anna, Arabella, Archie, Ashley...the list went on and on! ...Zac, Zara, Zeb, Zoe, Zybil.

(Zybil? That must be a spelling mistake, surely!)

Finally, Santa had delivered the
last present on his long Australian list.

"Great moons and stars!" sighed
Santa. "It's nearly morning and my sack seems as
heavy as ever! I hope I haven't forgotten anyone."

Santa opened his sack to check...but it was full
of juicy, crunchy carrots!

Santa divided the carrots among all the reindeer.
"Well, done!" he said, patting the youngest reindeer gently on the nose.

But the youngest reindeer didn't hear him...
he was too busy munching!

It was time to set off for home. Santa reset his Santa-nav once
more to the North Pole, and soon they were speeding away from
Australia, crossing the Equator, over Asia and through the rapidly
approaching dawn.